BUTCHERY AT THE DEBAUCHERY

BY

Eidahs

COVER BY

BINKY INK

BINKY INK

THE LITERARY ARM OF BINKY PRODUCTIONS

WWW.BINKYPRODUCTIONS.COM/SHORTSTORIES

<u>WARNINGS:</u>

*Strong Language, Mature Sexual Subject Matter,
Blood, Violence.*

Table of Contents

Part 1 7
Part 2 12
Part 3 19
Part 4 23
Part 5 28
Excerpt from *Sanguine Sincerity* 43
Also By 55
About the Author 56

<h1 style="text-align:center"><u>PART 1</u></h1>

Lakeshore Motel, 4:15 a.m.

Eric woke up to the noxious smell of vomit wafting up his nostrils. He blinked his drowsiness away, lifting himself from the couch, and looked around at his frat brothers sprawled all over the motel room.

'Oh, gross!' His eyes landed on a puddle of puke mere inches from where he stood.

Carefully lifting his feet, he walked over to the chair where he had set down his jacket. He looked it over – it was clean and his wallet wasn't missing. Breathing a sigh of relief after sifting through his wallet, he put his jacket on.

Eric Baker, the forensics major.
Age: 20; 5'8". Caucasian; brown hair cropped below the ears, short jawline beard, green-grey eyes.
Single.

The blonde mid-thirties babe on the bed next to two of his snoring friends rolled over, reaching for a half-smoked cigarette from the ashtray and lit it up, head upside down, staring right at him.

Be'linda, the sex worker.
Age: 37; 5'7". Caucasian; blonde hair, long to the middle of her back, tied in a stylish ponytail, blue eyes.
Relationship status unknown.

'Hey pretty boy,' she smiled. 'Never got your go at me last night. Not too late to take me on if you want.'

'Thanks, but, I, uh,' he tried not to stare at her large and very plump breasts. 'I prefer them younger.' She scowled. 'As in more my age!' he specified.

'Suit yourself, pretty boy, but your friends did pay me for the lot of you.'

An umber arm wrapped itself around her, and a baritone voice murmured, 'If he won't have a go at you, I'll take round two.'

Without replying, the sex worker took another puff of smoke and exhaled into Jared's mouth before claiming his tongue.

Jared Higgins, the quarterback.
Age: 21; 6'1". Jamaican descent; black hair, long jawline stubble and moustache stubble, dark eyes.
Relationship Status: ever-changing.

Eric let out a slow breath. 'Anyone want breakfast?' he called out.

'At 4:15 in the morning?' complained another of his boys, whose face was buried under the pillow beneath which he was sleeping.

'No? Fine, I'm going to get a snack.'

With a loud 'oof,' he exited the motel room, leaving the remnants of the debauchery behind him, and breathed in the fresh crisp spring air. Celebrating the seniors' upcoming graduation early had not been his idea, but he had gone along with it. He chuckled to himself. The night had been one hell of a rager.

He walked over to the door of the room next door and knocked. 'You two awake in there?' he called out. 'And decent?'

'Just about!' The door opened to reveal Dave and Juan who were in the middle of getting dressed. 'Party not raging anymore?'

Dave De Luca, the science major, and major geek, down to the glasses.
Age: 19; 5'9". Caucasian; brown hair, jawline beard and subtle moustache, brown eyes.
In a relationship with Juan.

Juan Gutierrez, the salsa dancer, and dance major.
Age: 18; 5'8". Castelian; black hair, five o'clock shadow moustache, grey eyes.
In a relationship with Dave.

'No, everyone is sleeping or doing Be'linda again,' replied Eric. 'Thought I'd make my escape and go hunt for food or something. Care to join me?'

'Sure, just give us a sec.' Dave pulled his shirt over his head, grabbing his things as Juan tied his belt.

'You two had fun after I left you to it?' Eric asked, grinning teasingly. 'You nearly forgot I was there for a moment.'

'Or maybe,' began Dave, 'we did it on purpose so my boyfriend and I could get rid of you.' He playfully shoved Eric.

'Yeah, yeah. At least we seem to be the three most sober ones, or less hung over.'

'Night's still young,' said Juan, shutting the door behind him. 'Maybe Dave and I merely had an interlude, *sí*?' He wiggled his eyebrows. 'And now we're going to chug the rest of that awful canned alcohol you Americans call beer.' He laughed. 'Next time, I'm having you drink *real cerveza*.'

'Let's see if Cameron, Drew, and Steven are up,' suggested Eric. 'They went off with the younger call girl.'

'So, how *was* the call girl?' asked Dave. 'The older one.'

Eric jerked his head up. 'Why? Not like either of you are interested in women.'

'Who says we aren't considering giving it a try?' teased Juan. He muttered something in Spanish into Dave's ear that sounded sensual.

'Because I know my two best buddies are too damn jealous of each other to be willing to try a threesome with *anyone*,' replied Eric, draping his arms around each of their shoulders as they started towards the next door over.

'You got us there,' laughed Dave.

'You think they're up?' asked Eric, pointing a thumb at the room – the blinds were shut.

'Light's still on,' observed Dave.

'At least the music is not blaring anymore,' noted Juan. '*¡Maldita sea*, was it loud.'

Eric knocked on the door and it creaked open a bit. 'That's not normal,' he said.

A rancid smell flooded his nose.

'Oh, dude, that's nasty!' cried Dave.

'Why does it smell like someone died in there?' Juan complained into his elbow.

Eric slowly pushed the door open. Immediately his eyes landed on the blood pooled on the carpeted floor and the three bodies strewn across it, and his stomach tightened. 'Because they did.'

<u>PART 2</u>

Lakeshore Motel, 5:00 a.m.

Eric paced to and fro, doing his best to quell the waves of nausea that threatened to make him spill whatever contents were in his already very empty stomach.

Juan was comforting Dave whose face was streaked with tears. Drew had been his brother, and not just any brother – his twin.

Dave had screamed his brother's name, wanting to rush to his side, but Eric and Juan had held him back, knowing there was nothing they could do now but call the cops.

The crime scene investigators had already taped the area off, as sirens continued to sound, and were getting ready to question everyone – if anyone could remember anything from last night, that was.

Eric looked over through the crack in the doorway as someone was placing a numbered yellow tag near Cameron's hand, and this time, it was a wave of sadness and anger that washed over him.

Drew De Luca, the swimmer.
Age: 19; 5'9". Caucasian; brown hair, clean shave, brown eyes. Dave's twin brother.
In a relationship with Fanny.
Murder victim.

Cameron Robinson, the English major.
Age: 18; 5'7". Caucasian, from a rich family of Brits; dirty blond hair, clean shave, hazel eyes.
Single.
Murder victim.

Steven Auclair, the film major, and social media influencer.
Age: 21; 6'0". Caucasian; dark brown hair, short beard and moustache, green eyes.
Relationship status: open, poly.
Murder victim.

A woman walked up to Eric, holding out her badge.
'Detective Hinata Kikuchi, Crime Scene Investigation. You the guy majoring in forensics who called us up?'
'I am.'

Hinata Kikuchi, the detective, crime scene investigator.
Age: 35; 5'5". Japanese; black shoulder-length hair, obsidian eyes.
Married.

Eric passed a hand through his hair. 'Fuck,' he breathed.

'Take it easy, kid. It's not every day you have a rager in a motel, only to find a triple homicide involving your friends. But you're the most sober of the group, and the one who called this in – figured we'd start with you.'

'And . . . I know how this works,' concluded Eric. 'I'm sober, the most lucid, the one who called it in, the one who moved around a bit. I'm your prime suspect, and I get it. So do what you gotta do, swab me, take my prints, check under my nails, do all you have to.' He locked eyes with her. 'I want to help – how ever I can. I'm graduating in just a couple of months. I know how this works,' he repeated.

'You're too close to the—'

'I don't care!' Eric pointed towards the room. 'Those guys were my friends, one of them my best friend's twin. Please, I *need* to be able to help. Please, just let me do this!' Eric's voice cracked as his desperation mounted. 'I just . . . I need to know who did this to them and why!' He blinked back tears.

'Okay, look, I'll talk to my team and my superiors and see if we can give you access as an intern, but you'll have to sign the paperwork – and I mean, *read through it thoroughly* before you sign it. We also need to process you completely to rule you out before you do anything else.'

'Whatever it takes, I'll do it. Process me.'

Detective Kikuchi gave him a sympathetic smile. 'All right.' She got a cotton swab ready and Eric opened his mouth to accept it.

* * *

Lakeshore Motel, 9:15 a.m.

After being processed, questioned, and scrutinised, Eric was given restrictive access to the case, meaning he could help the detectives question his friends, piece together the order of events from the previous night, *and* Kikuchi promised to let him in on some of their findings *if* he followed all their rules.

So far, what they had in terms of a series of events was this: everyone had been in the same room until 2:00 a.m., that's when the call girls arrived. Cam, Drew and Steven left with the youngest of the women and grabbed their own room, where they played blaring music long past 3:00 a.m. according to Dave and Juan, whose room Eric left around 2:45 a.m.

Eric walked over to Reception and chatted with the guy on duty to pass the time, which was confirmed by the guy in question. Eric then returned to the main room around 3:30 a.m., feeling tired, and sat on the couch, despite the shouts going on in the room, and his eyes shut on their own. He awoke moments before 4:15 a.m., which was when he left the room again. He, Dave and Juan found the bodies around 4:30 a.m.

It was past 9:00 now. Everyone was awake, had sobered up, dressed, and was muttering in sadness.

Everyone was accounted for, except for the younger sex worker.

Oh, and Fanny was there. Dave had called her.

Fanny Manning, the cheerleader.
Age: 19; 5'9". Bi-racial; black hair in braids, dark brown eyes.
Was dating Drew.

'I told you,' she shrieked, 'I left him!'

Eric walked over to where Fanny was laying into Dave.

'Fanny,' he placed a hand on her arm, 'it's not Dave's fault what happened to Drew.'

'You mean what Drew did to me!' corrected Fanny.

She turned and gave Eric's hand an appreciative squeeze. 'Eric, you know I'll always be good with you and Dave, but Drew . . .' She sighed. 'He butt-called me while he was fucking that hooker.'

'Shit, Fanny, I'm so sorry.'

Fanny whirled on Dave. 'Why didn't you stop him? Huh?'

'Would it have made a difference knowing he still wanted to hook up with a prostitute?' Dave asked defensively. Fanny shook her head. 'I have to live with the fact that I was having sex with my boyfriend while my twin brother was being murdered in the room right next to ours.'

Fanny's face fell. 'Dave . . .'

Dave sighed as Juan rubbed his arm, looking grim. 'I know you're going through hell right now, Fanny, but so am I.'

'I know. I'm sorry I blamed you.'

'I get it,' said Dave. He and Fanny hugged it out, allowing themselves to weep together for a few minutes before Fanny pulled away.

'How about you walk us through what happened, Fanny,' suggested Eric.

'I texted Derek to find out where you all were,' Fanny answered, 'to know what was up with the Triple D's gang and their boys. Derek told me Dave, Juan and you had left the party after call girls had arrived and that he saw Drew, Cam, and Steven leave with one of them. So I came right over, saw them through the window.' Her face contorted in anger. 'I kicked that door open!'

Eric could believe it. Fanny was the strongest in the cheerleading team.

'I screamed at him for cheating on me, because you know what I found when I walked in?'

'I'm guessing Drew cheating on you,' replied Eric.

'Drew's cock inside *her* mouth, while Cam was in her ass and Steven in her vagina!'

'Yeah, I'm sorry,' Eric said softly.

'I told him, "We are over! We're finished, we're done!"' Fanny's eyes widened. 'And you know what he said? He told me to wait. He started *explaining*. And then he *came inside her mouth!* Right in front of me!!'

'A little T.M.I., but, yeah, that's rough,' voiced Juan.

'And the music that was playing?' asked Eric.

'You mean that noise that was blaring like death metal? I don't know who picked that music out, but the door was wide open when I stormed out of there.'

'Where did you go afterwards?' asked Detective Kikuchi, walking over. 'I imagine you needed someone?'

'I went home. You can ask my grandma, she was there wiping my snot as I cried into her lap.' Fanny heaved a sigh. Eric was uncertain as to what to say.

Detective Kikuchi signalled Eric to follow her. He obliged. 'I know Fanny didn't do it,' Eric blurted. 'I believe her.'

'That's not for you to judge, Mister Baker.'

Kikuchi's team ran over to her and began whispering frantically. 'We found blood from a fourth source,' one of them said. 'We're having it processed now.'

'Evidence suggests a struggle with the perpetrator,' another one informed them.

'They fought back,' whispered Eric. Of course, they would have! Yet, as he imagined his friends fighting for their lives with no one able to hear their cries, the weight of it felt heavier on his shoulders now.

<u>PART 3</u>

Lakeshore Motel, 9:45 a.m.

While Detective Kikuchi and her team conferred for a bit, Eric sat in the seedy motel's room, packed in with all his friends and Be'linda.

Fanny was crying into her hands as Derek was stroking her back in attempt to comfort her. 'I kept telling you, Fanny, Drew's no good for you.'

Derek Slovenski, the barista.
Age: 22; 5'8". Caucasian; brown short flowing
hair, long stubble, blue eyes.
Single.

'I should've listened to you,' Fanny wept.

Derek sighed. 'I wish you would have called me . . . or at least let me know you were here. You *know* I would do anything for you.'

Fanny looked up into Derek's eyes. 'You don't hate me for choosing him over you?'

Derek shook his head. 'You chose him, I respected that, but I'm not gonna pretend like it didn't break my heart.' He stared down at his shoes. 'I hate that he's dead. I feel icky wanting to take his ex from him like this, but Fanny,' he lifted her chin to meet his gaze, 'I'll be here if and when you're ready for me.'

Fanny offered him a wan smile, wiping her eyes. 'I just need time, okay? But Derek . . .' She bit her lower lip nervously. 'Thanks.'

Fanny leaned into Derek's embrace.

'The love triangle that was,' sighed Leo, sitting next to Eric.

Leo Rodriguez, the T.A.
Age: 18; 5'9". Mexican; short curly hair, stylish pinch and moustache, brown eyes, round glasses, long chin.
Single.

He passed a hand through his hair. 'I keep wracking my brain trying to remember what happened last night. I remember Be'linda, thank the heavens I remember the wonderful things she did to me—'

'Uh, T.M.I.,' Kyong warned, sitting down beside them.

Kyong Eun, the photographer.
Age: 20; 5'8". Korean; long shoulder-length black hair, clean shave, dark eyes.
Single.

'My point is, I'm glad I remember that part. But after? I got too drunk to remember anything.'

'You were singing at the top of your lungs,' said Kyong. 'And dancing on top of the dresser before Jared picked you up and carried you around the room.'

'You remember?' asked Eric.

Kyong let out a mirthless laugh. 'As if. But I took photos all night. Photos I thought would be great for those of us graduating and to print to post all over the dorm's walls.' He sighed.

'Let me guess,' began Eric, 'Kikuchi and her team confiscated your camera.'

'And all the photos I took last night.' Kyong looked pained. 'Some of them were my best work. I took great pics, with the perfect depth of field.'

'Chin up, my friend,' said Leo, sounding cheerful, though it seemed strained, 'you'll get it back.'

'Nah,' said Jared as he joined them, 'you ain't seeing that thing ever again; it's evidence. Heard the detective saying so to her team.'

'Who do you think did it, Jared?' asked Leo, sobering.

Kyong slapped his arm. 'Not so loud, Leo; Dave's right there. A little sensitivity.'

'Well, it can't be any of us,' said Jared. 'Yeah, we got spliced and we trashed the place, but we're bros, man. We look out for each other. None of us would *ever* . . . do . . . kill . . .' He gave up as the words escaped him, looking somewhere between anguished and sorrowful.

'Did they . . . was there . . . a struggle?' Kyong asked gently.

'Yeah,' said Eric. 'Evidence points to that. Stab wounds and lacerations mostly. It was . . .' He put a hand to his mouth.

Leo rubbed his back. 'Sorry. You're right Kyong, we shouldn't speculate—'

'All right, listen up!' Detective Kikuchi called out. 'We received confirmation regarding blood from a fourth source from the murder scene, blood we believe belongs to our perpetrator.' She paused deliberately. 'A *male* perpetrator.'

A hush fell in the room, and Eric's heart sank. Could one of his friends truly have murdered three of their own frat boys?

'I know we swabbed you all,' Kikuchi went on, 'but now we're *processing* you . . . *One. By. One.*'

Part 4

Lakeshore Motel, 11:00 a.m.

'Can I go?' complained Be'linda. 'You know it wasn't me who did it.'

'We'll question you next and if your story checks out, then you're clear to go,' Kikuchi said. 'The rest of you, get in a line along that wall and no one moves or leaves this room without my say-so. Understood?'

'Understood,' the guys muttered responses, some of them with more conviction than others.

Eric glanced at Dave and Juan. He jogged over to Kikuchi. 'Does that include me?'

'No, you were cleared hours ago, so you're going to help us question the sex worker while my colleagues process your friends. Sorry, I can't let you process them.'

'I get that, but do you really think it's necessary to keep Dave and Juan here? I mean,' Eric lowered his voice, 'Drew was Dave's twin.'

'Just following protocol, Mister Baker. Now follow it too if you wanna stay on this case.'

Eric sighed but followed Kikuchi without complaint to where Be'linda sat smoking a cigarette by the window, her elbows on the table that stood there. Sitting down across from her, Kikuchi slapped a folder on the table and opened it up to show papers that had information about Be'linda and some illegal activities with drugs she had been a part of.

'No,' Be'linda sighed, leaning over to look at the files, 'Be-linda, with an apostrophe.' She took a puff of smoke. 'Look, I don't know why y'all are questioning *me*. I've got half a dozen alibis right in this room.'

'Because your colleague was with the murder victims and now she's fled from the scene,' replied Kikuchi. 'This is a triple homicide, ma'am.'

'Tori's a sweet girl, she wouldn't hurt a fly,' said Be'linda. 'And you said yourself, the perpetrator is male.'

Tori Almeida, the other sex worker.
Age: 23; 5'6". Brazilian; short neck-length black
hair, amber eyes.
Relationship status unknown.

'She could have called in back-up,' suggested Kikuchi. 'Young woman, three strong drunk men, all fun and games until one of them becomes aggressive in their drunkenness and she calls for a friend or two to come help her out. Wouldn't be the first time.'

Kikuchi pointed at the mention of an incident in the file when Tori had called Be'linda and their boss, who had arrived and threatened the two men Tori had been entertaining.

'That was one time, and we didn't touch them,' said Be'linda, taking a drag from her cigarette. She exhaled while she spoke, the smoke forming a small cloud in front of her. 'I do my job, which is to entertain clients in whatever sexual ways they desire of me. I don't touch anyone who doesn't want me to touch them and I only touch folks the way they want me to touch them.'

'*I* know that,' said Eric, 'and *you* know that.' He pointed at Kikuchi and her partner behind her. 'Them?' He made a face. 'How about we give Tori a call? Make sure she's okay. My friend's girlfriend did come shouting at them while Tori was there. I'm sure that was upsetting for your friend.'

'Yeah, Tori's not tough like us more seasoned sex workers are. Still gets upset over exes and girlfriends catching their men cheating. All she wants is to provide pleasure, you know? Not get between lovers.'

'I get that,' said Eric. He looked to Kikuchi, who nodded. Her partner handed Be'linda her phone.

Be'linda dialled but frowned when there was no answer. 'Hey sweetie, it's me. You left early after the foursome. How'd that go? Your first foursome, eh? Was it all you had expected? Gimme a call back.' She hung up. 'I'll try our boss. We have to report back all the time anyway.'

'Put it on speaker,' Kikuchi instructed.

Be'linda rolled her eyes but obliged.

'Yes, Be'linda, what can I do you for?'

'Yeah, Greg, you know that amazing frat party Tori and I came to entertain?'

'Yes, the one that's going to make us a ton of money?'

'That's the one. Listen, Tori left early, not sure if she was feeling unwell with all the excitement from the boys. Did she say anything to you about it?'

'Tori hasn't been in,' replied Greg. 'I thought she was still there with you. But you know who *was* here, though? Matt.'

'Not that stalking son of a bitch!' hissed Be'linda.

'Who's Matt?' Kikuchi asked, her voice just above a whisper.

'Tori's stalker,' replied Be'linda.

Matt Henton, the stalker.
Age: 43; 5'9". Caucasian; shaved head, long stubble, muscular build, stern face, possesses many scars.
Single.

'You know what he looks like?' asked Kikuchi.

Be'linda nodded, closed the call with her boss, and gave Matt's description and full name to Kikuchi, who called her lab. 'That blood from that fourth source? Run it through CODIS.'

Eric waited as Kikuchi remained on the line. Then he heard it. 'Confirmed match! Matt Henton. Arrested for stalking and harassing on multiple counts. No murder charges.'

'Perhaps not, but he's got motive and he left his blood behind.' Kikuchi rose to her feet, hurrying to the door and securing her gun as she announced. 'This isn't just a triple homicide anymore, we've got a missing witness who could be our perpetrator's next victim.' She paused, lowering her voice. 'This just turned into a missing person's case.'

<u>PART 5</u>

Lakeshore Motel, 11:30 a.m.

The room was abuzz with frantic whispers as more from Detective Kikuchi's team arrived to process the scene and let the guys go free. Be'linda was arguing that she should tag along with the cops, and Eric couldn't agree more.

'She knows Tori, and she knows this Matt guy too. She can help us,' he insisted.

'Who said *you* were coming along?' Kikuchi asked condescendingly. 'This case just took a new turn. You're a forensics major, kid. Your internship ends here.'

'But my friends are dead!' shouted Eric. He sensed his frat brothers gather around him.

'I want to accompany you too,' expressed Dave, his voice solemn. 'I want to look into the eyes of the man who killed my twin and ask him why.'

'You know why,' Juan said gently.

Dave balled his hands into fists. 'I want to see him go down for what he did.'

'And that's precisely why I can't let you,' declared Kikuchi. 'Go home, boys. All of you. Let me do my job.'

Kikuchi's team began escorting everyone out of the motel room.

Eric turned to them. 'We need food. Let's go grab a bite to eat.' He widened his eyes, hoping they would get his meaning. 'Be'linda, lunch is on me.'

Eric turned to Kikuchi. 'Detective Kikuchi, thank you for the opportunity to help with . . .' He trailed off.

'We're going to find your friends' murderer, I promise,' she asserted.

Eric nodded and the group of friends walked away from the motel. Once they were out of earshot, Eric turned to them, walking backwards.

'Okay, so we do need food. We can't hunt a murderer on an empty stomach.'

'That son of a bitch is going to see his end if I have anything to say about it,' Dave seethed.

'I know I just broke up with him,' Fanny began, 'but I want justice too.'

'And we'll get it,' said Derek, 'for all three of them.'

'Be'linda, you're our best shot at finding this Matt guy. Is there anything you know about him that might lead us to him?' asked Eric.

'The first time Tori had him as a client, it was a dual service – I was with her,' replied Be'linda.

'Do you remember where that was?' asked Leo. Be'linda confirmed.

Eric nodded. They spoke a bit more about their plan before grabbing something quick to eat at a diner.

It wasn't that Eric was hungry per se, he was still feeling unwell from the shock of what happened, but they all needed sustenance. Not to mention no one had taken any of their cars – those who *could* drive – given they all knew they'd be getting trashed at the party. They'd have to high-tail it in a cab or by foot.

Eric was glad to see Be'linda and Fanny talking jovially enough. The older woman was showing sympathy towards Fanny, who in turn expressed not hating Tori, only hating that Drew had cheated on her, and Be'linda acknowledged the younger woman's whirlwind of emotions.

'All right,' said Kyong. 'I might have gotten my camera confiscated, but Steven and I always helped each other a lot and he taught me how to isolate sound. I still have my phone, and I've got apps on it.'

'Uh, dude, we've all got apps on our phones,' said Leo.

Kyong ignored him. 'Send me your videos and I can try to see what I can pick up from them that might give us a clue of when everything happened.'

'You sure that's a good idea?' asked Eric. He glanced over at Dave.

'It's an excellent idea,' confirmed Dave, as he sent Kyong a video he'd taken of Juan teasing him flirtatiously in their motel room.

They took a few moments as Kyong did his thing, trying to dampen sound to boost something or other Eric wasn't certain about. Meanwhile, Be'linda called her fellow sex workers and her boss, and got everyone on high alert regarding Tori. She jotted down all the places Tori had met with Matt before he had begun stalking and harassing her.

'That's where we'll start.' said Be'linda, 'It's gotta be one of these places.'

'I've got something,' announced Kyong.

They settled in a quiet alley as Kyong put the volume high on speaker. The originally blaring music had been dampened, so it was lower.

A muffled male voice muttered something inaudible and a woman's voice shrieked.

'Get the hell out!' Tori screamed, which came through clipped after Kyong had processed it.

Then Eric heard it, sounds of fighting – punches, grunts, a cry from Cameron, a gurgle, Steven's shout being cut off abruptly, and Drew's voice ringing out for help. Tori had screamed again and Matt had shouted after her. Heavy boots left the scene. Then all there was, was the blaring music and someone crying out for help until his voice grew too faint to hear – Drew.

Dave put a hand to his mouth – his entire body was trembling, he could barely stand. Juan was rocking him back and forth. Everyone's expressions were solemn.

'I think I know where he took Tori, of all these places,' said Be'linda.

Eric nodded and the others cried out their anger as they followed Be'linda through the city.

* * *

Seedy Apartment, 12:15 p.m.

They came to a seedy, rundown apartment block and entered, bounding up the stairs two at a time.

'This is where many drug deals go down,' explained Be'linda. 'No one ever questions any violence that happens here.'

A high-pitched muffled scream tore through the corridor.

'Tori!' Be'linda ran down the corridor towards the apartment where the shout had come from.

Eric pulled his phone out and dialled Kikuchi's number. 'We've found her!' He gave the address and prayed Kikuchi would arrive soon.

'We've gotta do something,' Jared urged, cracking his knuckles.

'We've gotta wait for the cops!' Leo advised emphatically.

'No, Tori's in there, she could die!' cried Be'linda.

'That guy killed three of our friends!' insisted Leo. 'He can kill the rest of us.'

'Not all of us!' growled Jared.

'Drew was a swimmer, and strong, Steven was a big and heavy guy with large muscles, and Cameron was fast, despite his skinniness. And that maniac – one man – killed all three of them . . . And then kidnapped Tori. How can you possibly think that you or any of us can take him on!'

Jared paused, breathing heavily, contemplating.

It was Dave who answered. 'Because we . . . have rage.' He kicked the door so hard it busted open on the first try.

'What the fuck!' shouted Matt, hunkering towards the door, looking like the muscular skinhead he was.

He stopped as the group pushed past the doorway and his eyes narrowed on Dave.

'You killed my brother,' seethed Dave.

Tori was bound to a chair, blindfolded and gagged. She looked like she had been roughed up.

Jared stepped forward, towering over Matt.

'Careful,' Eric warned.

Behind him, Kyong and Leo stood at the ready but a bit behind for backup. Eric realised they could get arrested for what they were doing, all of them, but it was worth it if they saved Tori and got out of it unscathed.

Matt laughed, his ugly face contorting. 'You think a bunch of college students can intimidate me?'

Fanny and Derek retreated a few steps with Leo and Kyong. Juan whispered something to Dave as Eric tensed up.

Matt lifted a large fist and Jared blocked it with his hand, pushing against the hulking man. The two began exchanging blows. Dave jumped in, kicking Matt in the shin.

Be'linda ran past the fighting men, Eric at her heels. Together, they unbound Tori and freed her of her gag and blindfolds. The younger woman's breathing was erratic, panicked, and tears were in her wide eyes.

'It's okay, Tori, we've got you. We're getting you out of here.'

'No, you're not!' Matt growled.

Eric turned and tasted dirt as a boot landed on his mouth, sending him tumbling to the floor. The ladies shrieked but ran out of the way, retreating behind Leo and Kyong who took protective stances in front of them.

When Eric looked up again, Matt was whipping out four knives, two in each hand at an angle from each other.

He slashed towards Jared who ducked. Derek joined the fray. Fanny cried out to him. 'Don't!'

Jared landed a blow to the stalker's stomach and turned in time as a fist came at him – Matt swiped at his face with one of the knives. The jock was merely grazed.

Many of the others stood alert but uncertain as to how to jump in with Matt waving his knives about furiously fast – anytime someone tried to get close to attack him, they risked getting their throats sliced or a vital part stabbed. It was impossible to penetrate his defences.

Dave screamed in rage, kicking Matt's hand and one of the knives fell from his hand. Matt dove towards Dave, head first, and drove a knife into his leg. Juan screamed as Dave fell to the floor.

Dave planted a knee on the floor, plucking the knife out of his thigh, and slowly rose to his feet, the whole time glaring dangerously at Matt, bloody knife in hand. The man came at him again and punched Dave's face, breaking his glasses.

'Dave!' Juan ran in, grabbing his arm to pull him back, but Dave merely shrugged him off him.

'You killed my twin,' seethed Dave. 'Now you're going to die.'

Matt laughed sinisterly. 'Come at me, then, young man, if you think you've got what it takes. After all, I took down two of your friends in one go, sliced the throat of one of them, stabbed the other multiple times, and your brother? I left him to bleed out.'

'Aargh!' Dave screamed hoarsely as he ran towards Matt, knife held high. He stopped short when Matt punched him in the gut with a fistful of knives, and he grunted.

'Dave!' shouted Juan, tears already pouring down his face.

Jared didn't wait, he came at Matt and kicked him in the face, taking him off guard. Eric pounced on him from behind as Derek kicked his flank, and the stalker dropped his other knives as he attempted to swipe at Eric. Derek kicked the fallen knives across the floor.

Dave staggered back into Juan's arms, clutching at his stomach, but there was no blood. Dave grinned menacingly as he steadied himself and lifted his shirt to reveal his thick phone.

'Next time someone teases me for having such a bulky phone, remember it saved my life today.'

Juan gaped at Dave, who walked towards Matt as everyone else pinned him to the floor. Dave loomed above Matt, shaking as he gripped the knife so hard his knuckles turned white. He bent and placed the knife at Matt's throat.

'Do it!' Matt taunted. He laughed sinisterly. 'Watch me bleed out and know that your brother bled out longer before he died.'

Dave's face contorted in rage and sorrow before he pulled his hand back and threw the knife across the room, screaming in rage. He punched Matt in the face, letting out another guttural scream.

'Put the weapon down, Mister De Luca!'

Dave took a step back from Matt, hands in the air as Detective Kikuchi and her team stormed the apartment, guns raised.

'I don't have any weapons.' Dave presented his hands. He indicated the blood from his wound, wincing, and a medic began bandaging his thigh.

Kikuchi gave Eric a stern look. 'I thought I told you all to—'

'They found me and saved me!' exclaimed Tori. 'They're all heroes, every last one of them.'

Kikuchi sighed as she holstered her gun – everyone else on her team continued to train their weapons at Matt, as they took over from the boys to hold him down. One of the officers pressed her gun to Matt's head as her colleague grabbed the stalker's arms and yanked them behind his back.

'Evidence, Mister Eun.' Kikuchi held out her hand to Kyong.

'Damnit!'

The cops handcuffed the seized Matt, who grumbled and grunted.

'This isn't over, Tori,' he shouted as he was being dragged out. 'You're mine! You're fucking mine!'

Dave collapsed, trembling, and Jared caught him before he could fall. The medic helped steady him as well.

Dave looked at Juan, both of them weeping openly, and the two men's mouths crashed together in a passionate kiss before they wrapped their arms around each other. Everyone gathered around them and joined the embrace.

Eric moved to join them as well before Kikuchi stopped him.

'Look,' she sighed, 'unofficially, you all did well, you stubborn and brave rule-breakers. Officially, I'm going to have to give you all a warning.'

Eric smiled mildly, feeling adrenaline leaving his body. 'We did what we had to. For Drew, for Cameron, for Steven.'

He glanced over at his friends, who had included Be'linda and Tori in their hug. They were all laughing out of relief, even as they were sobbing and trying to hide it, now that it was over and the murderer of three of their fraternity brothers had been apprehended.

Without another word, Eric joined his friends, tears stinging his eyes. Dave had a hand on his eyes, sobbing loudly, Juan wept into his boyfriend's neck. Fanny cried with Derek, holding hands for support, while Leo and Kyong wept silently. Jared heaved his chagrin, and Be'linda and Tori cried out of relief.

A sob escaped Eric's mouth, and he reached out to Dave, who took his hand and held it tightly. And the ten of them remained that way, holding each other as they grieved for their murdered friends.

<u>THANK YOU SO MUCH FOR READING</u>

If you enjoyed this story,
please consider taking a few moments
to write a review on Amazon or Goodreads.
It would mean so much.

Thank you.

Please enjoy this passage from

Sanguine Sincerity

The first book in an ongoing series of
Supernatural LGBTQ Erotic Romance Thriller
books.

THE EXCERPT IS CLEAN.

Warnings:
Strong language, violence and blood.

<u>Chapter One</u>

Present Day.

The silence was both terrifying and soothing at the same time. Liam closed his eyes and leaned against the brick wall as he stood outside the club. It had been busy, with people dancing, shouting, laughing, all drunkenly. Now, the stillness of the winter night dampened whatever sounds came from the boulevard a few streets down.

This was where he had often stood with Julian after their work shifts, talking, laughing, kissing, and making plans for their future together. But Julian was gone, left before dawn a few nights after they had declared their love for each other, left without a word or explanation. Only a scribble on a sticky note saying, *'I have to leave. I'm sorry.'*

It hurt, it still did, even after all these weeks. Julian had never called or answered Liam's calls or texts after that night; Julian had simply disappeared from Liam's life. Liam didn't understand why – he thought they'd been happy.

He had once relished in the quiet after the bustle of work, now he missed hearing Julian's voice or seeing his smile. His heart broke every day again and again. Yet he continued to stand here in the spot they had made theirs.

Liam couldn't help but wonder if things had moved too fast between them – no, he had declared his love six full months after they'd met and started dating. He was just so confused about it all.

Taking a deep breath, he ensured the club was well locked and began down the dark alley. He didn't want to linger too long. There had been murders in the neighbourhood in recent weeks, all gunshot wounds. The rival gangs were at it again. It hadn't stopped the clubgoers, though. Liam figured it was only a matter of time before both mobs decided they wanted to own the club and took their fight to the neighbouring streets.

Liam heard the screech of tires and shouting not too far. He paused, waiting to make sure it was just some drunk folks, but he tensed when he heard a gunshot pierce the stillness.

Looks like the gang fight's here now, he thought to himself.

He quickened his pace and veered the corner into the next alley and came face to face with the man who had left him.

'Julian!' Liam breathed. He swallowed hard, his heart suddenly drumming in his chest.

'Liam.' Julian hesitated. His blue eyes seemed brighter in the darkness of the night and the light in the alley gave his already pale complexion a blue hue, making his handsome features that much more intense, increasing the yearning and anguish in Liam's heart.

Liam was flooded by a wave of emotions. 'What the hell, Julian?' he shouted, tears stinging his eyes.

Julian winced, chagrined, and Liam saw his eyes sparkle with tears.

'Look,' began Julian, taking a step towards Liam, 'I know I owe you an explanation, I just . . . You need to get out of here. I came to get you to safety.'

Liam took a step back, putting two and two together. 'I know what this is,' he seethed. 'You're with the mafias, aren't you?'

'No, I swear, Liam! I'm not with them,' protested Julian. 'I heard about the Cromwells and Sharpes taking their fight here and I came to warn you. Liam, please.' Julian reached for Liam's hand.

Liam pulled away out of reach. 'A little convenient, isn't it?'

Julian grimaced. 'Liam, I promise you—'

'Promise me? I told you I loved you and then you ran!' shouted Liam, his voice hoarse with heartache. His heart felt tight, and it hurt all over again.

Julian merely gaped at him.

'I thought you loved me too,' Liam wept.

'I do. I do *still* love you,' insisted Julian.

'Then why did you leave?' demanded Liam.

'I had . . . priorities.' He caught himself. 'Sorry, that sounds . . . I had . . . a mission.'

'A mission?' Liam repeated, incredulous. 'Crime mission? Or are you with the cops?'

'None of those,' admitted Julian. 'Look, I promise I'll explain everything. Let's just get out of here, go somewhere safe, and I'll explain everything.' He paused and a tear trickled down his cheek – he wiped it away with the back of his thumb. 'I just ask that you trust me.'

'You left, Julian.' The tightness in Liam's chest squeezed harder. 'You claim you love me but you left – why come back now?'

Julian stared at Liam, eyes pleading. 'I had no choice, something . . . took me away for a while, and I realise I should have told you then what it was and why that was, because—'

Gunshot thundering too close for comfort interrupted their tearful exchange.

Julian grabbed Liam's hand and began to run, pulling Liam along with him. 'We have to get out of here. I'm not going to let any harm come to you.'

'Oh, how noble!' spat Liam.

Julian spun on Liam, glaring at him. 'I came back as soon as my mission was complete. I always intended to. I just couldn't tell you then and it's . . . difficult to explain, it would be difficult for you to belie—'

With surprising speed, Julian placed his hand in front of Liam and pushed him against the wall, backing up as a bullet whizzed past them.

Liam stared at Julian, mouth agape. 'Thanks.'

Julian took a beat, looking alarmed, before grabbing hold of Liam's hand again and guiding him out of the alley and bolting onto the street. Shouts coming from nearby told them which way *not* to run as they turned onto the next street over, darting as fast as they could.

Some of the mobsters ran onto the street where they were. Julian skidded to a stop, his eyes darting this way and that, looking hypervigilant. He grabbed Liam's arm and pulled him close, turning around as one of the gang members took aim at them. They ducked behind a parked car.

'We're not with the Sharpes!' Julian shouted. Liam noted how Julian had easily recognised that the ones shooting at them were the Cromwells.

In response, the shooter reloaded his gun.

'Shit!' Julian cursed. He looked towards another parked car. 'If we can get ourselves out of this area,' he told Liam, 'then we—'

The window of the car behind which they hid shattered as another shot resounded behind them.

They ran towards the next car, and then towards another building. Another thunderous roar broke the air as more gang members began shooting at each other. Liam and Julian's assailant continued after them and just as they came up to hide in an alcove, a bullet hit Julian with a thud.

He cried out in pain, bringing his hand to his arm.

'Julian!' Liam cried.

Julian closed his eyes, wincing. 'I'll be fine,' he gritted. He looked over at Liam as they leaned against the wall. 'I'm sorry I never told you the truth. I'm sorry

I left – I'm sorry I hurt you. But I swear I love you and I will tell you *everything*. We just need to get to safety.'

Liam nodded. 'You knew they were coming here. I just can't wrap my head around—'

'I found out just hours ago.' Julian looked at his wound, breathing deeply but looking like the pain wasn't as intense now as it was before. 'I got myself here as quickly as I could.'

'You came to . . . warn me . . .' Liam was just so confused. 'Please, tell me if you're part of a gang of some sort.'

'Of some sort,' Julian repeated pensively. 'Not a mafia, no. Not a . . . It's complicated.' Julian pinched his fingers and reached into his wound and pulled out the bullet with nothing more than a small groan. 'I'm good.'

Suddenly, the barrel of a handgun emerged from the corner – the shooter was pointing it straight at Julian's head, his grip on the handgun firm and steady.

Liam froze.

Julian stared the other man in the eyes. 'Big mistake,' he sneered.

With exceptional speed, he grabbed the assailant's arm, pulling and twisting. The Cromwell crony cried out, dropping the gun, and Julian grabbed his neck and twisted hard. The man fell dead on the ground before him.

Liam stared at Julian. 'And you say you're not a cop or with a mob,' he said, unconvinced. He pointed at the dead shooter, his eyes never leaving Julian's. 'Explain that!'

'Not here.'

Julian picked up the dead man's gun and began to run; Liam followed close behind. A car turned onto the street and mobsters began to shoot at anyone who was nearby.

'Fuck!' Julian shouted. Shielding Liam as they continued to run, Julian took aim and began shooting at the mobsters within the vehicle, hitting his mark every time.

'Now I know there's definitely something you're not telling me,' Liam muttered as they ran.

'There is, and I promise I'll tell you,' replied Julian. He secured the clip and aimed afresh, again not missing his target.

Liam's throat and lungs were burning but he pushed forward. They turned another corner as the car behind them crashed into a fence.

Liam stopped before Julian, facing him. 'The truth now, Julian!'

Panting, Julian stared at Liam. 'We need to get away from here,' he insisted.

'I'm not moving until you tell me what's going on.'

Fear flashed in Julian's eyes. 'You're not going to believe me without the full explanation.'

'Then quit stalling and explain already!' demanded Liam.

Julian worked his jaw. 'I'm—'

A deafening gunshot exploded – Liam felt a sharp, burning sensation in his gut, and his knees buckled beneath him as he struggled to stay upright.

'No!' screamed Julian.

He caught Liam before he could hit the ground, gently setting him down. Liam's breath came out syncopated as he realised what had just happened. He screamed in pain – a loud guttural scream – then winced, clenching his jaw.

'No, no, this is what I was trying to prevent,' Julian quavered, opening up Liam's jacket and staring at the wound. 'I can't lose you.'

'Lose me? You left me.'

Julian let out a tearful breath. 'I left on a mission I couldn't tell you about. I'm so sorry, Liam.'

Liam glanced down at his stomach as his blood rapidly drenched his clothes. Seeing it only made his heart pump harder and the blood gush faster, and Liam's breath came out shakily.

Julian pulled Liam close to his chest, picking him up off the ground, and began to run. Liam didn't know if it was the dizziness of blood loss that altered his perceptions but he felt like they were moving a lot faster than was normal. He saw houses whizz by his vision and then trees as they entered the forest. The sounds of guns and shouting mobsters grew distant until, finally, the quiet of the night was all that remained.

Julian placed Liam down on the snow, which quickly turned red from his blood. Julian's jaw was clenched.

The pain Liam felt was immeasurable, yet somehow he couldn't bring himself to scream again, and he was so sweat-soaked from fear, he barely noticed the cold.

'I should never have waited this long to tell you the truth, Liam.' Julian looked down at Liam's wound, his tears dripping onto it.

Liam tried to speak but a mere whimper escaped him as tears stung his eyes.

Julian's voice came out determined yet half-whispered. 'I'm not going to let you die.'

'I think,' Liam winced, his voice laboured, 'it's too late for that.'

'No!' Something flashed in Julian's eyes. Liam lifted a bloodied hand to Julian's face; Julian placed his hand on his. 'I came back because I love you . . . because I owe you the truth. So here is the truth.'

His eyes flashed again and paled, brightening, his pupils becoming as blue as his irises and nearly as pale. He let his mouth hang open, and smoothly his top canines extended. Liam's eyes widened and he gaped at Julian.

'You're a—' he gasped.

'Yes. I can save your life, but tell me no and I won't, as much as that grieves me. I won't force this life on you.'

Liam gritted his teeth as a wave of pain threatened to pull him into unconsciousness. 'Do it!'

Julian leaned down towards him and gently placed his teeth on his skin. He paused. Liam felt Julian's breath on his neck before an intense sting.

He winced, grabbing Julian's arm tightly. He felt Julian's lips wrap around the punctures and the pain eased. As Julian sucked his blood, Liam relaxed in his caress.

Julian kissed Liam's neck tenderly before pulling away. 'It's done,' he said softly.

Liam waited, his body trembling lightly. Then he began to shake, but not from pain, from some sort of power that coursed through his veins. It was a vibration that came from inside of him that he felt gushing through all his veins. In his mouth, Liam felt his eyeteeth extend, and there was a mild prickle in his eyes that he just knew was the same kind of flare he'd seen in Julian's eyes.

Liam looked down at his wound, feeling an uncomfortable sensation. The bullet appeared at the opening of the hole in his stomach and fell out. Then the wound closed and Liam felt himself heal inside his body. It wasn't pleasant but the discomfort quickly passed.

Liam swallowed hard, breathing in deeply. He stared at Julian.

He wasn't sure which of them sprung towards the other first but their lips met and their mouths opened to let the other in, and they kissed fervently. The familiar tingling in Liam's stomach told him how much he loved and wanted Julian.

He pulled away. Julian leaned his forehead on his.

'I am so sorry, Liam, that I never told you the truth.'

'You should have trusted that I'd believe you,' Liam placed his hand on Julian's face, 'that I'd still love you despite who or what you are.' Liam grimaced at the blood he'd smeared on Julian who didn't seem to mind.

Julian kissed Liam again. 'I love you, Liam. I promise I'll never leave your side again.'

Liam let that sink in, realising the implications of this new situation. 'I guess that means we're geared to spend eternity together.'

Julian's lips quirked into a side grin. 'Is that a proposal?'

Liam chuckled, feeling flutters all over his body. 'It is if you want it to be.'

Julian beamed at him, and with his heightened senses Liam could feel the truth and their love reverberate and pulse between them.

Liam pressed a long and ardent kiss to Julian's lips, wrapping his arms around him, deepening the kiss with each passing moment, and his tongue traced his lover's vampiric canines as they hungrily devoured each other's mouths.

Liam drew back and met Julian's gaze. 'You owe me one hell of an explanation.'

Julian let out a small laugh. 'That, I do.'

Julian helped Liam to his feet and he beckoned him to follow. He held out his hand and Liam took it, interlacing their fingers. They walked through the snow in the forest, the silence of the night no longer terrifying Liam, and Julian's voice soothingly cut through the stillness as he began his story.

Eidahs is a pseudonym for all mature written works, from thrillers to erotic romance. Eidahs in pronunciation sounds elven in nature, which is why she chose it, to tap into her love of fantasy, a genre that couples well with super-natural and preternatural, dark fantasy, and romance.

Eidahs is also the nickname 'Shadie' backwards, repre-senting the shadow self, innermost desires, and a spectrum of emotions, most notably, passion, sorrow, rage, and delight, which Eidahs loves to incorporate in her writing. Enticing readers and evoking the characters' emotions when she writes has guided her inspiration to spell many short stories on Medium and a series of books under this pen name.

Connect with Binky Ink:

WordPress Website & Blog
https://binkyproductions.com/binkyinkwriting
Medium – Main Profile
https://medium.com/@BinkyInkWriting
X (Twitter) https://twitter.com/binkyinkwriting

www.ingramcontent.com/pod-product-compliance
Lightning Source LLC
Chambersburg PA
CBHW071358200726
48294CB00004B/1216